Clyde Monster

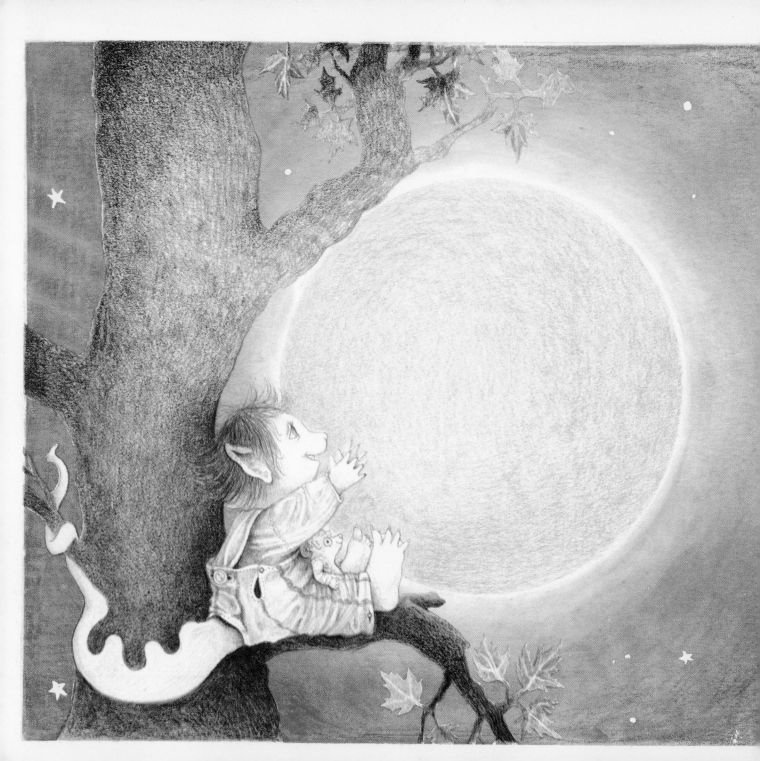

Clyde Monster

by Robert L. Crowe

illustrated by Kay Chorao

A Puffin Unicorn

Unicorn is a registered trademark of Dutton Children's Books.

Library of Congress number 76-10733

ISBN 0-14-054743-6

Published in the United States by
Dutton Children's Books, a division of
Penguin Books USA Inc.

Editor: Ann Durell   Designer: Riki Levinson

Printed in Hong Kong by South China Printing Co.
First Unicorn Edition 1987   W
10 9

Clyde wasn't very old, but he was growing—uglier every day. He lived in a large forest with his parents.

Father Monster was a big, big monster and very ugly, which was good. Friends and family usually make fun of a pretty monster. Mother Monster was even uglier and greatly admired. All in all, they were a picture family—as monsters go.

Clyde lived in a cave. That is, he was
supposed to live in a cave, at night anyway.
During the day, he played in the forest,
doing typical monster things like breathing
fire at the lake to make the steam rise.

He also did typical Clyde things like turning somersaults that made large holes in the ground, and generally bumping into things. He was more clumsy than the average monster.

At night, Clyde was supposed to go to his cave and sleep. That's when the trouble started. He refused to go to his cave.

"Why?" asked his mother. "Why won't you go to your cave?"

"Because," answered Clyde, "I'm afraid of the dark."

"Afraid," snorted his father until his nose burned. "A monster of mine afraid? What are you afraid of?"

"People," said Clyde. "I'm afraid there are people in there who will get me."

"That's silly," said his father. "Come, I'll show you." He breathed a huge burst of fire that lit up the cave. "There. Did you see any people?"

"No," answered Clyde. "But they may be hiding under a rock and they'll jump out and get me after I'm asleep."

"That is silly," pointed out his mother with her pointed tongue. "There are no people here. Besides, if there were, they wouldn't hurt you."

"They wouldn't?" asked Clyde.

"No," said his mother. "Would you ever hide in the dark under a bed or in a closet to scare a human boy or girl?"

"Of course not!" exclaimed Clyde, upset that his mother would even think of such a thing.

"Well, people won't hide and scare you either.
A long time ago monsters and people made a deal,"
explained his father. "Monsters don't scare people—
and people don't scare monsters."

"Are you sure?" Clyde asked.

"Absolutely," said his mother. "Do you know of
a monster who was ever frightened by a people?"

"No," answered Clyde after some thought.

"Do you know of any boys or girls who were
ever frightened by a monster?"

"No," he answered quickly.

"There!" said his mother. "Now off to bed."

"And no more nonsense about being scared
by people," ordered his father.

"Okay," said Clyde, as he stumbled into the cave. "But, could you leave the rock open just a little?"

ROBERT L. CROWE is Superintendent of Schools in Jacksonville, Illinois. He has also taught English and speech, and been a school director of personnel. *Clyde* came into being to help his own children when they went through a stage of being afraid of the dark, and he hopes the story will provide assistance as well as enjoyment for other families.

KAY CHORAO is the illustrator of many picture books, including *Tyler Toad and the Thunder* by Robert L. Crowe and *Albert's Toothache* by Barbara Williams. Ms. Chorao says that she has a special empathy for the theme of *Clyde Monster* because she spent her entire fifth summer sleeping with her head buried under a pillow to keep out what she feared might be behind the draperies in the bedroom of a new home. Ms. Chorao and her family live in New York City.